HEiDi HECKELBECK

and the Cookie Contest

By Wanda Coven

Illustrated by Priscilla Burris

LITTLE SIMON

New York London Toronto Sydney New Delhi

LITTLE SIMON

An imprint of Simon & Schuster Children's Publishing Division
1230 Avenue of the Americas, New York, New York 10020
Copyright © 2012 by Simon & Schuster, Inc.
All rights reserved, including the right of reproduction in whole or in part in any form.
LITTLE SIMON is a registered trademark of Simon & Schuster, Inc., and associated colophon is a trademark of Simon & Schuster, Inc.
For information about special discounts for bulk purchases, please contact Simon & Schuster Special Sales at 1-866-506-1949 or business@simonandschuster.com.
The Simon & Schuster Speakers Bureau can bring authors to your live event. For more information or to book an event contact the Simon & Schuster Speakers Bureau at 1-866-248-3049 or visit our website at www.simonspeakers.com.
Manufactured in the United States of America 1015 MTN
10
Library of Congress Cataloging-in-Publication Data
Coven, Wanda.
Heidi Heckelbeck and the cookie contest / by Wanda Coven ; illustrated by Priscilla Burris.
p. cm.
Summary: Heidi wants to win the Brewster Elementary cookie contest, but does not think through all the consequences of adding magic to her recipe.
ISBN 978-1-4424-4165-1 (pbk. : alk. paper) — ISBN 978-1-4424-4166-8 (hardcover : alk. paper) — ISBN 978-1-4424-4167-5 (e-book : alk. paper)
[1. Witches—Fiction. 2. Magic—Fiction. 3. Contests—Fiction. 4. Cookies—Fiction. 5. Schools—Fiction.] I. Burris, Priscilla, ill. II. Title.
PZ7.C83392Hb 2012
[Fic]—dc23
2011017223

CONTENTS

ME WANT COO-KiE!

Yum!

Yummy!

Yummers!

Heidi Heckelbeck had cookies on her mind. She had just signed up for the Brewster Elementary cookie contest. Heidi had never entered a contest before. She wondered if she would win. She had won a raffle one time, but that had been super-easy. All she'd had to do was write her name on a strip of paper and stick it in a box with some other names.

The prize had been a silver turtle necklace. Winning had been fun, and now, more than anything, Heidi wanted to win the school cookie contest.

What kind of cookies should I make? wondered Heidi. She could make oatmeal raisin, but raisins were kind of squishy and gross. Peanut butter cookies were good, but not her favorite. *How about chocolate chunk?*

Chocolate chunk would be a winner, thought Heidi. They were also her favorite.

Heidi hopped onto a step stool and grabbed the family recipe box from the cupboard. She found the tab marked "Desserts" and thumbed through the recipes.

"Aha!" said Heidi out loud.

"Aha, what?" asked Heidi's mom as she walked into the kitchen.

"I found our famous chocolate chunk cookie recipe," said Heidi. "I entered a cookie contest at school. It's this Saturday."

"Need some help?" asked Mom.

"Do I EVER," said Heidi. "I've never made cookies all by myself."

"Let's gather the ingredients first," said Mom.

Henry, Heidi's five-year-old brother, ran into the kitchen. "Can I help?"

"No," said Heidi firmly. "These cookies have to be made by ME."

"Then can I be your taste-tester?" asked Henry.

"Ha! Are you kidding?" asked Heidi. "That would be like hiring the Cookie Monster."

Then Henry pretended to be the Cookie Monster.

"Me want COO-kie! Munch! Munch! Chomp! Chomp!"

Heidi rolled her eyes. Then she looked at the recipe. "Three cups of flour," she said.

Heidi lugged a tub of flour from

the pantry and plopped it on the counter. Mom got the white sugar, brown sugar, and chocolate chunks. Heidi got two sticks of butter from the fridge. They laid out all the ingredients on the counter. Then Mom got the mixer, the measuring spoons, and the measuring cups.

"Oh no," said Heidi. "We're out of eggs."

"That's okay," said Mom. "I'll pick some eggs up on the way home from school tomorrow. If we make the cookies in the evening, they'll be nice and fresh for the contest the next day."

"Good idea," said Heidi.

"So, what do you get if you win?" asked Henry.

"You get to have your picture and your recipe published in the town newspaper," said Heidi.

"That's it?" said Henry. "No cash prizes or giveaways?"

"Well, there IS one giveaway," said

Heidi. "The winner can *give away* her brother for a year of free cookies."

"Ha-ha. Very funny," said Henry. "But if you gave me away, you would probably miss me."

"Maybe a teeny bit," said Heidi.

Henry smiled. "Does that mean the taste-tester gets to have his picture in the paper too?"

"Don't push it, little dude," said Heidi.

Chapter 2

BA-BA-BORING!

At school everybody was talking about the cookie contest. Stanley Stonewrecker was going to make Heavenly Surprise cookies. Charlie Chen was going to make toasted s'mores cookies. Natalie Newman was going to make pumpkin whoopie pies with cream cheese filling. *Wow,* thought Heidi as she put her things in her cubby. *Everyone else's cookies sound so fancy.* Heidi began to wonder if her cookies were special enough.

Heidi walked over to her friend Lucy Lancaster. "What kind are *you* making?" Heidi asked Lucy.

"Sugar cookies," said Lucy. "With Fruity Polka Dots cereal on top."

"Yum," said Heidi.

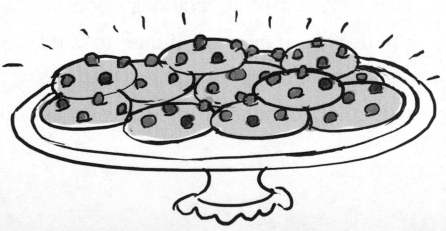

"What kind are *you* making?" asked Lucy.

"Chocolate chunk," said Heidi.

"Ew," said Melanie Maplethorpe.

Melanie was Heidi's worst enemy. She had been listening in.

Heidi turned around. "What's your problem?" she asked.

"YOUR COOKIES!" said Melanie. "I mean, how blah can you get? Even Girl Scout cookies are more exciting than THAT."

Lucy put her hands on her hips and glared at Melanie. "What kind are *you* going to make?" asked Lucy. "Disgusting chip? Or oatmeal poison?"

"Neither," said Melanie. "I'm going to make cinnamon swirl cookies with toffee bits. My ingredients had to be *special ordered*. And by the way, I'm SO going to win."

Then Melanie did a little twirl and walked off with her nose in the air.

"Well, whoop-de-do," said Lucy to Melanie's bouncing ponytail.

Heidi sighed. "It's true," she said. "My chocolate chunk cookies DO sound boring next to yours and Melanie's."

"Chocolate chunk cookies are NOT boring," said Lucy. "Stick with what you do best and you'll come out on top."

On top of what? thought Heidi. *The garbage heap? Hmm . . . Maybe I need to come up with a fancier kind of cookie.*

A few minutes later Heidi's teacher, Mrs. Welli, handed out contest rules and entry forms. Heidi decided to give her boring cookies a new name. On her entry form, she wrote, "Magical Chocolate Chunk Cookies." *That sounds a teeny bit better than plain chocolate chunk,* she thought. Then she handed it in.

ENTRY FORM   NAME: Heidi Heckelbeck

COOKIE NAME:

Magical Chocolate Chunk Cookies

Later in gym, Heidi's class did the Wacky Obstacle Course. Bruce Bickerson and Heidi were partners. Together, they jumped through a pretend flaming hoop. They walked the balance beam over a pit of crocodiles. They zip-lined across a steep valley. In the middle of the *Indiana Jones*

snake-filled tunnel, Heidi asked Bruce what kind of cookies he was going to make for the contest on Saturday.

"Mega Mint," said Bruce. "They're chocolate cookies with vanilla chips and crushed peppermints."

"Wow," said Heidi. "They sound amazing."

"They're insane," said Bruce. "But some people think they taste like toothpaste."

Heidi didn't think Bruce's cookies sounded anything like toothpaste. They sounded mega-tasty. Everybody's cookies sounded great except hers. There was no way crummy ol' chocolate chunk cookies would win the contest. She had to come up with something new—something different. *But what?* thought Heidi as she crawled out of the tunnel and lined up with her classmates.

Heidi was sure of one thing: She just *had* to outshine Melanie Maplethorpe. That mean girl didn't deserve to win anything.

Chapter 3

RAZZLE-DAZZLE!

When Heidi got home, she raided the pantry. She grabbed pretzels, mini marshmallows, jelly beans, a box of old candy canes, and Peanut Butter Crunch cereal. She piled everything onto the counter with her other cookie ingredients.

"What are you doing?" asked Henry.

"Jazzing up my cookie recipe."

"What for?"

"So I can beat Melanie," replied Heidi. "She's making cinnamon swirl cookies with toffee bits."

"Do they taste good?" asked Henry.

"She had to SPECIAL ORDER her ingredients," said Heidi.

"But do they *taste good*?"

"How should *I* know?" said Heidi.

"Maybe they're gross."

"I doubt it," said Heidi. "Everything Smell-a-nie does is perfect."

"But OUR chocolate chunk cookie recipe is perfect too," said Henry.

Heidi folded her arms and looked at Henry. "Melanie laughed when she heard I was going to make chocolate chunk cookies."

"Has she tasted our cookies?"

"No."

"She should," said Henry. "They're

the best-tasting cookies in the whole world."

"Who made YOU a cookie judge?"

"I did," said Henry.

"But you like animal crackers," said Heidi. "A real cookie judge would know that animal crackers are not good cookies."

"They're called animal CRACKERS. They're not even cookies. Besides, I can tell the difference between a good cookie and a bad cookie."

"Well, I want to make a blue-ribbon cookie," said Heidi.

"Then you should make our Heckelbeck Chocolate Chunk Cookies," said Henry. "They're the BEST!"

"You said it!" said Mom.

"Let's get started!" said Dad.

Heidi's mom and dad had walked into the kitchen during Heidi and Henry's discussion. Her parents both had on aprons. Dad handed an apron to Heidi. Heidi had never worn an apron before. She took the apron and slipped it over her head. Mom tied the sash in the back. All of a sudden Heidi began to feel like a real cook.

Now all she had to do was make a first-place, blue-ribbon cookie.

Chapter 4

DAD FAINTS

Heidi's dad switched on the oven. Then he pointed at the pretzels, candy, and cereal sitting on the counter.

"What's all this?" asked Dad.

"Magical ingredients," said Heidi.

"Heidi wants to jazz up the family cookie recipe," said Henry.

Dad was puzzled. "What for?"

"Because it's SO blah," said Heidi.

Dad pretended to faint into Mom's arms. Mom struggled to hold him up.

"Heidi, look what you've done to your father," said Mom.

"What did she do?" asked Henry.

Heidi looked at her dad.

He opened one eye and peeked at Heidi. Then he coughed and sputtered.

"I just want to add a little zing," said Heidi. "What's the big deal?"

Dad stood and rolled up his sleeves. "Is that the *real* reason you want to add junk food to our cookies?" he asked.

Heidi looked at the floor.

"Do you think our recipe is missing something?" asked Dad.

"Bingo," said Heidi.

Dad was surprised. "Heidi, this

is not just *any* recipe. I've worked on it for *years*. These cookies are something special."

Heidi still looked doubtful. "What makes them so special?"

"Let me show you," said Dad. He switched on the stove. "First we need to brown the butter."

"What's so special about that?" asked Heidi.

"Wait and see," said Dad.

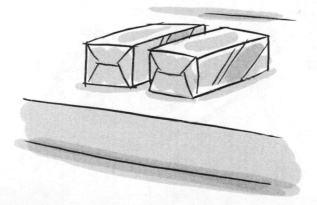

Heidi unwrapped the butter and dropped them into a pan. Soon the butter began to sizzle. Heidi stirred it around. After a while the butter began to bubble. Dad took it off the flame.

"Smell," said Dad.

Heidi and Henry both sniffed the browned butter.

"Smells good," said Heidi.

"Like toffee," said Henry.

"Exactly," said Dad. "Browning the butter gives the cookies a toasty toffee flavor. That makes them stand apart from other chocolate chunk cookies."

Heidi beat the browned butter, the sugars, the flour, and the vanilla. She cracked two eggs into the batter and mixed them in. Dad added an extra yolk to the bowl.

"An extra yolk will make them soft and chewy," said Dad.

Heidi swirled in the yolk.

"I also add two kinds of chocolate," said Dad. "Milk chocolate and semi-sweet. That's another special twist."

Heidi yawned. Dad's special steps

didn't sound very exciting. If he had asked her to add some chopped-up candy bars and rainbow sprinkles, *that* would've sounded exciting.

Dad handed Heidi an ice-cream scoop. She scooped the cookie dough and squeezed the handle. Mounds of dough plopped onto the greased cookie sheet.

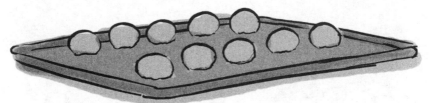

"Now we'll bake them at a very high heat," said Dad. "And we'll only cook them for four minutes. This will make them golden on the outside and like cookie dough on the inside."

Heidi set the timer for four minutes. Then she and Henry stood on two chairs and watched the cookies bake.

Dad got out fancy dessert plates. Mom laid out napkins. When the cookies were done, Heidi slid one onto each plate.

Then it was time to taste them.

They all took a bite at the same time.

"Mmmmmmmm," everyone said. Everyone—except Heidi, that is.

Chapter 5

THE MAGIC TOUCH

Honk . . . shoooo!

Honk . . . shoooo!

Snoresville, USA.

Heidi carried the rest of her sample cookie to her bedroom on a napkin. She still thought the recipe was B.O.R.I.N.G., but she wanted to think about it alone. She flopped onto her beanbag chair. *Am I being unfair?* she wondered. After all, Dad *did* work on soda recipes for a living. He must know *something*. Heidi studied her cookie. It gave her an idea. What if

she pretended to be a professional cookie judge? Then she could judge the cookie fairly. Maybe she would see it in a new way.

Heidi fished around in her backpack and pulled out the contest rules.

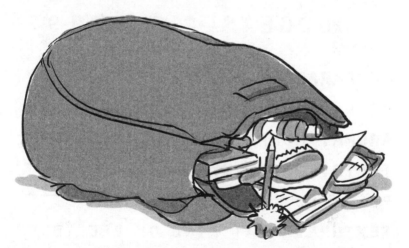

At the bottom of the page she found the Judge's Checklist. Heidi grabbed a

scented pencil from her pencil case.
It had a sugar cookie smell. Then she
looked at the scorecard.

Scorecard ✓

JUDGE'S CHECKLIST

APPEARANCE: WHAT DOES THE COOKIE
LOOK LIKE?
AROMA: HOW DOES THE COOKIE SMELL?
TASTE: DOES THE COOKIE HAVE A
PLEASING TASTE?
TEXTURE: WHAT KIND OF FEEL DOES
THE COOKIE HAVE?
CREATIVITY: WHAT MAKES THIS
COOKIE STAND OUT?

A judge has to be super-honest, thought Heidi. Then she took a good, hard look at her cookie. *Hmmm, how does this cookie look?* she asked herself. She tried to pretend she was judging somebody else's cookie.

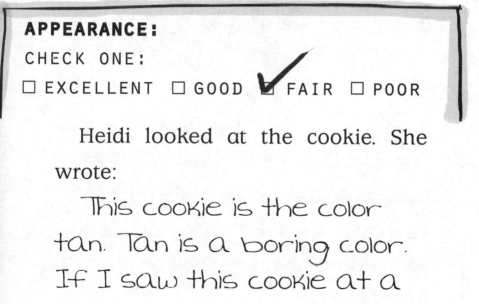

APPEARANCE:

CHECK ONE:

☐ EXCELLENT ☐ GOOD ☑ FAIR ☐ POOR

Heidi looked at the cookie. She wrote:

This cookie is the color tan. Tan is a boring color. If I saw this cookie at a bakery, I would say, "NEXT!"

Heidi sniffed the cookie and wrote:

This cookie does not smell like dead fish—that's the good news! The bad news is that it smells like a plain ol' everyday chocolate chunk cookie.

Heidi took a bite of her cookie. She thought hard about how it tasted. Then she wrote:

Thankfully, this cookie does not taste like liver. It tastes ho-hum. Who hasn't tasted a chocolate chunk cookie before?

Heidi took another bite of her cookie and thought about the feeling of the cookie. Then she wrote:

This cookie is not rubbery or slimy or anything gross. It's crisp on the outside and chewy on the inside with little bursts of chocolate.

See, Heidi said to herself, *I'm being fair and honest. I found something good to say about this cookie.*

The last question was the hardest.

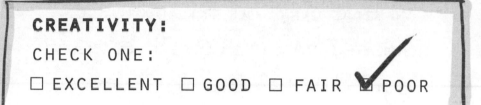

CREATIVITY:

CHECK ONE:

☐ EXCELLENT ☐ GOOD ☐ FAIR ☑ POOR

Heidi stared at what was left of her cookie. Then she wrote:

This cookie lacks pizzazz. Where are all the wow-ee colors? Where are the zany ingredients? It's not even a fun shape. What this cookie needs is a touch of magic.

Suddenly Heidi's eyes lit up.

"THAT'S IT!" she shouted. "All my cookie needs is a magic touch!"

THE COOKiE CHARM

Zip!

Zap!

Zing!

Heidi pulled her *Book of Spells* out from under her bed. She flipped through the pages and found a chapter called "Zesty Recipe Makeovers."

"NOW we're talking," said Heidi.

Then she noticed the perfect spell.

The Cookie Charm

Are your cookies ho-hum? Do they have the look and feel of a hockey puck? Are you the kind of witch who burns your cookies to a crisp? Then this is the spell for you! No ovens! No pans! No mess! No fuss!

60

It was called The Cookie Charm.

She read it over.

Ingredients:
Your baked cookies
Your favorite additional
cookie ingredients
1 cup vegetable oil
2 teaspoons pure vanilla
A dash of nutmeg

61

Put your baked cookies in an empty container. Add the vegetable oil, vanilla, nutmeg, and favorite cookie ingredients. Hold your Witches of Westwick medallion in your left hand.

Place your right hand over the mix. Chant the following words:

WITH THIS POTION
MY PLAN GOES INTO MOTION.
SOON YOU WILL EAT
A SUPER-TASTY TREAT!

Cover and let sit for
12 hours. Enjoy!

Heidi shoved her *Book of Spells* under her pillow. Then she cracked open the door. She could hear Mom helping Henry in the tub.

She crept downstairs and peeked around the corner. Dad was reading by the fire. She snuck into the kitchen

and pulled a shopping bag from the cupboard. Heidi placed the tin of chocolate chunk cookies in the bag. Then she tiptoed into the pantry and grabbed the jelly beans and mini marshmallows. Next she gathered the other spell ingredients, along with a teaspoon and a measuring cup. She dumped everything in the shopping bag.

Now what else can I add? Heidi wondered. *I know!* She opened the fridge and grabbed a chunk of cheese.

Now, THIS is what I call zing, she thought as she dropped it into her bag.

"Ahem!"

Heidi froze.

Oh no! she thought. *I'm SO busted!*

But no one was there. It had only been Dad clearing his throat in the other room. *Phew,* thought Heidi. Then she zoomed to her room and locked the door.

Heidi laid her spell ingredients

on the floor. She opened the tin of chocolate chunk cookies. Then she poured the spell ingredients on top. *They look more colorful already!* thought Heidi. *My cookies are going to blow Smell-a-nie's cookies away!*

Heidi put on her medallion. She held it in her left hand and put her right hand over the mix. Then she chanted the spell. The cookies began to bubble. Heidi covered them and looked at the clock. It was nine p.m. The cookies would be done in twelve

hours—that would make it nine in the morning. *Perfect,* thought Heidi. *The contest is at eleven.* Heidi snuck into the kitchen and put back the tin of cookies, teaspoon, and measuring cup. She was ready for the contest. Now she had to get ready for bed.

Chapter 7

P.U.

Heidi's eyes popped open. It was nine o'clock on the dot! That meant her spell was all done! She hopped out of bed and ran to the kitchen in her kitty cat pajamas. She pulled the lid off of the cookie tin and peeked at her cookies.

Wow! she thought. *It WORKED!*

Heidi's cookies had a beautiful shape—round and plump. The jelly beans, marshmallows, and chocolate looked like they had been perfectly placed. The swirls of cheese added a nice touch. There was only one thing that was a little odd: the smell.

"P.U.," said Heidi, waving her hand in front of her nose.

She closed the lid. *Well, no big deal,* she thought. *My nose isn't used*

to smelling cookies first thing in the morning. Plus I'm still sleepy. I'm sure my cookies are okay. They definitely LOOK amazing! They might even win!

"Hey, missy," said Mom, who had just walked into the kitchen with Henry. "Are you sneaking cookies before breakfast?"

Heidi jumped. "No way. I was just making sure Henry hadn't snuck any."

"Are you calling me a thief?" asked Henry.

"Well, it wouldn't be the first time," said Heidi.

"Cool it, you two," said Mom. "Or there won't be any surprise."

"Surprise?" questioned Heidi.

"What surprise?" asked Henry.

"Dad got doughnuts for breakfast," said Mom.

Heidi and Henry looked around the kitchen and spotted a pink box on the counter.

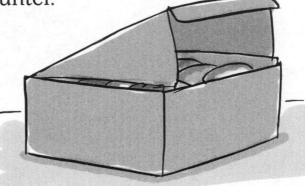

"I get the rainbow sprinkles one!" said Heidi, running for the box.

"I get the twisty kind!" said Henry, right behind her.

"I'll get the plates!" said Mom.

Mom put plates on the table. She also brought over an empty silver tray and a doily.

"What's that for?" asked Heidi.

"It's for your cookie display," said Mom.

"Fancy," said Heidi as she sank her teeth into a soft, sweet doughnut.

"We can set up the cookies on the tray when we get there," said Mom.

"When can we leave?" asked Heidi.

"As soon as everyone's ready," said Mom.

After breakfast Heidi put on her green skirt and her T-shirt with silver stars. Then she pulled on her black-and-white-striped tights and

black sneakers. Heidi looked in the mirror. She wondered what it would feel like to win first place. She practiced a winning smile in the mirror.

"Time to go!" called Dad.

Heidi thundered down the stairs, grabbed her tin of blue-ribbon cookies, and jumped into the car.

Chapter 8

STiNK! STANK! STUNK!

A large white party tent had been set up in the middle of Brewster Elementary's playing field. There were also two smaller tents—one for sign-in and another to sell drinks. All the tents had balloons hanging inside and out. A banner across the front of the big tent read BREWSTER ELEMENTARY COOKIE CONTEST.

Heidi could see the judges' table underneath the big tent. It had a red-and-white-checked tablecloth with ruffles around the bottom. There were three chairs behind the table—one for each judge. On either side of the

judges' table were the display tables. *Wow*, thought Heidi. *This is a BIG deal.*

Heidi ran to the sign-in tent. She got entry number twelve. Heidi slipped the ticket with her number into her pocket. Then she skipped to the display table with her family close behind. Mom set the silver tray on

the table and placed the doily on top.
Heidi opened her cookie tin. A funky
smell floated from the container.

Henry pinched his nose. "Ew.
What's that smell?"

"It's the smell of blue-ribbon
cookies," said Heidi proudly.

"It smells more like dog poop,"
said Henry.

"That's so funny I forgot to laugh,"

said Heidi as she began to place the cookies on the tray.

Heidi's mom and dad also took a step back from the cookies. Dad fanned his nose with his hand.

"What happened to the cookies?" asked Dad.

"I snazzed them up," said Heidi.

Mom raised an eyebrow. *"Heiii-di,"* she said slowly. "Just *how* did you snazz them up?"

"Oh, you know," said Heidi, avoiding the question.

Unfortunately, Mom *did* know.

"Heidi, you know the rule," Mom said firmly. "No witching skills in your everyday life."

Heidi sighed loudly. "But how else was I going to make my cookies better?"

Dad rolled his eyes. "You still don't get it, do you?" he said.

"Get what?" asked Heidi.

"Never mind," said Dad.

"All right, we'll talk about this later,"

said Mom. Then she changed the subject. "So, what kind of cheese did you use?"

"The one with the blue spots," said Heidi.

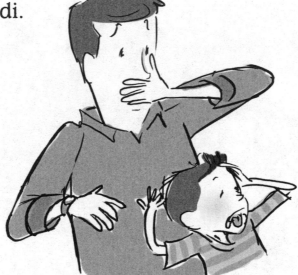

"The stinky cheese?" asked Dad.

"You mean the dog poop cheese!" said Henry.

"Stop it!" said Heidi. "I think my cookies look great."

"They *do* look great," said Mom. Then in a much lower voice she said, "But they stink to high heaven."

Heidi filled out a card with the name of her cookies and her entry number. She put it in front of her tray.

MAGICAL CHOCOLATE
CHUNK COOKIES

A Chocolate-y Chees-y
Marshmallow and Jelly Bean Delight

ENTRY NUMBER 12

"You forgot your name," said Henry.

"Did not," said Heidi. "The judges only allow entry numbers."

"Lucky for you!" said Henry.

"Why?" asked Heidi.

"Then no one will know that YOU brought the stinky cookies," said Henry.

★ ⋆ ✳ ◎ ⋆

I don't give one hoot what my family thinks about my cookies, thought Heidi as she looked for Lucy. Heidi spotted her setting up her cookies at another table. Melanie Maplethorpe was working right next to her.

"Hey, Lucy!" said Heidi.

"Hey," said Lucy.

"Where are the Fruity Polka Dots?" asked Heidi, looking over Lucy's cookies.

"I decided not to use them," said Lucy. "They tasted better plain."

"You made *plain* sugar cookies?" said Heidi.

"Yup," said Lucy. "Why? What's wrong?"

"I'll tell you what's wrong," said Melanie Maplethorpe, butting in. "They sound positively BOR-ing!"

Lucy looked crushed.

Heidi felt sorry for Lucy, but this time she kind of agreed with Melanie.

Plain sugar cookies did sound dull.
The Fruity Polka Dots cereal would
have put her cookies over the top.
Now Lucy had no chance of winning.
But Heidi didn't dare say anything.

She didn't want to hurt Lucy's feelings.

"Come on, Lucy," said Heidi. "Let's check out some of the other cookies."

Heidi and Lucy linked arms, and off they went.

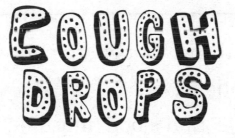

Chapter 9

COUGH DROPS

Heidi and Lucy waved at Bruce. He was standing beside Brewster's school bell. The bell ringer started the contest, and this year Bruce had been chosen to ring the bell. Principal Pennypacker's assistant, Mrs. Crosby, gave him the signal. Bruce pulled the string.

Bong!

Bong!

Bong!

The judges quickly took their seats. Mrs. Crosby tapped the top of the microphone.

"Hello and good morning, every-

one," she began. "Welcome to the annual Brewster Elementary Cookie Contest. Here are this year's superstar judges: Jennifer Childs, our town newspaper's food editor! Brewster Elementary's Principal Pennypacker! And Lou Billings, Brewster's mayor! Now, let the judging begin!"

Everyone clapped and whistled.

Heidi grabbed Lucy's hand and squeezed it. They watched as the judges sampled cookies and made notes on the scorecards. The judges kept straight faces when they tasted the cookies—even when they tasted Melanie's yummy-sounding cinnamon swirl cookies with toffee bits.

But when they got to Heidi's cook-ies, the judges began to make funny faces.

Suddenly the principal's eyes bugged out and he grabbed his throat.

The food editor from the *Brewster Daily* looked like she had eaten rat poison.

And the mayor of Brewster began
to have a coughing fit.

It got so bad that Mrs. Crosby had to
run and get a jug of water. The mayor
gulped the water straight from the jug.

"Heidi, did you put pepper in your
cookies?" asked Lucy.

"No," said Heidi.

"Then what's going on?"

"I dunno," said Heidi. "They kind of have a funny smell. . . ."

"Like what?" asked Lucy.

"Like stinky gym socks," said Heidi.

"How come your cookies smell like gym socks?" asked Lucy.

"Maybe it's the cheese," said Heidi. "I added cheese to the recipe."

"Oh, Heidi," said Lucy. "Why didn't you just stick with plain chocolate chunk?"

Heidi looked at the mayor. He was still gulping down water.

"I wanted my cookies to stand out," she said.

"Oh, they stand out all right," said Lucy.

The mayor finally stopped coughing. His face had turned bright red,
but he looked okay. Mrs. Crosby gave
him a cough drop. *Phew,* thought
Heidi. Then she told herself that it
was no big deal. Anyone could choke
on a cookie.

Right?

Chapter 10

The judges took FOREVER.

"I'm going bonkers," said Heidi.

"Me too," said Lucy.

"Do you think Melanie will win?"

"Probably," said Lucy.

"Hey, look!" said Heidi, pointing at one of the display tables.

"Oh my gosh!" said Lucy.

Bruce's dog, Frankie, had grabbed a tablecloth in his teeth. He tugged on it. The cookie trays inched toward the edge. He tugged again. A tray fell on the ground. Cookies scattered across the grass, and a girl screamed. It was

Melanie. Melanie tried to rescue her cookies, but Frankie was too fast. He scarfed them all down. Bruce grabbed Frankie and put him on his leash.

Heidi and Lucy burst out laughing and slapped each other five.

Then Mrs. Crosby stepped up with

the microphone. She waved a big white envelope in the air.

"We have a winner!" she said.

Everyone clapped and cheered.

Mrs. Crosby opened the envelope and pulled out the winning name.

"The winner of this year's cookie contest is . . ." She squinted at the name. "Lucy Lancaster!"

"WHAT?" cried Lucy.

The crowd burst into cheers.

Heidi almost fell over. *Not Lucy! How can plain sugar cookies win the contest? What is going on?* she wondered.

"Will Lucy please come forward?" asked Mrs. Crosby.

Heidi was still in shock, but she gave Lucy a great big hug. "Wow," she said. "Congratulations!"

"Thanks, Heidi!" said Lucy. "I can't believe it!"

Neither can I, thought Heidi.

Lucy walked to the judges' table. The judges were standing in front of the table with Mrs. Crosby. They took turns praising Lucy's first-place cookies.

"Simple, yet extraordinary," said Principal Pennypacker.

"A pleasing blend of ingredients," said the food editor.

"Crisp on the outside and tender on the inside," said the mayor. "I *must* have the recipe!"

Mrs. Crosby pinned a beautiful blue ribbon on Lucy's shirt.

Lucy posed with the principal and the mayor. A photographer snapped their picture. Heidi stared in disbelief. Her shoulders slumped. She felt like such a loser. Lucy had stuck with a simple recipe and come out on top.

Heidi had gone overboard and made the mayor gag. Mom, Dad, and Henry walked over and patted Heidi on the back.

Heidi moaned. "You were right," she said.

"You had to find out for yourself," said Dad.

"Boy, did I stink up your recipe," said Heidi.

"You certainly did," said Dad.

"They smelled like gym socks," said Heidi.

"Dog poop," said Henry.

"Moldy cheese," said Mom.

Heidi smiled. "Next year I won't change a thing."

"Hallelujah!" said Dad. Then he rubbed his hands together. "So, who wants to sample some cookies?"

"I do!" said Heidi.

"Me too!" said Mom.

"Let's go!" said Henry.

And then the Heckelbecks tasted the cookies—all of them except for Melanie's because, of course, they were all gone.

Woof!

Check out the next book starring

HEIDI HECKELBECK

HEIDI HECKELBECK in Disguise

HERE'S A SNEAK PEEK!

Heidi wanted to scream a million mean things in Melanie's face, but she felt totally tongue-tied. Heidi made her meanest face ever instead. But Melanie kept right on talking.

"So, Miss Weirdo, have you picked

An excerpt from *Heidi Heckelbeck in Disguise*

out a Halloween costume?"

"None of your business," said Heidi, trying to sound tough.

"Well, no need to bother," said Melanie. "Be what you are—a total NUT!"

"Melanie Maplethorpe!" said Lucy, with her hands on her hips. "If I looked up 'evil' in the dictionary, I'd find a picture of you."

"Why, thank you!" said Melanie. "That's the nicest thing anyone's said to me all day. And by the way," she added, turning to Heidi, "as long as we're playing Dictionary, we all know the definition of 'weirdo' is Heidi."

Heidi scrunched her fingers like the claws of a cat and swiped the air in front of her. *"Rrrear! Siss! Phtt! Phtt! Phtt!"*

"Wow," said Melanie. "You really ARE a weirdo!"

"Okay, that does it!" said Heidi. "Halloween is BACK ON!"

"What's that supposed to mean?" asked Melanie.

"You'll see," said Heidi.

Heidi didn't know exactly what she was going to do, but she was sure about two things: She was NOT a weirdo. . . . And she had to get a costume.

An excerpt from *Heidi Heckelbeck in Disguise*